PLEASE SAY PLEASE, GRUMPY BUNNY!

For Diane Namm, please stay as sweet and encouraging as you are!
—J.K.F.

For Rori, who always remembers to say please. Lots of love.
—L.M.

Text copyright © 2007 by Justine Korman Fontes
Illustrations copyright © 2007 by Lucinda McQueen

All rights reserved. Published by Scholastic Inc.
SCHOLASTIC and associated logos are trademarks and/or registered trademarks of Scholastic Inc.
GRUMPY BUNNY is a trademark of Scholastic Inc.

ISBN-13: 978-0-439-02012-1
ISBN-10: 0-439-02012-3

12 11 10 9 8 7 6 5 4   8 9 10 11 12/0

Printed in the U.S.A.
First printing, November 2007

PLEASE SAY PLEASE, GRUMPY BUNNY!

by Justine Korman Fontes

Illustrated by Lucinda McQueen

SCHOLASTIC INC.

New York   Toronto   London   Auckland   Sydney
Mexico City   New Delhi   Hong Kong   Buenos Aires

Chapter 1
The Magic Word

One morning, Mrs. Clover asked her class,
"Does anyone know the magic word?"
Hopper O'Hare's ears flew up.
A magic word!
Would it bring toys to life?
Or make bunnies fly?

No one could guess.
"The magic word is *please*,"
Mrs. Clover said.
Hopper's ears drooped.
He rolled his eyes.
The word *please* wasn't magical.
It was just one of those polite words
grown-ups fussed about,
like *thank you* and *excuse me*.

Hopper wasn't used to
saying please.
He was an only-bunny.
Hopper never had to ask brothers
or sisters for things.
And at Corny's crowded house,
everybunny was too busy playing
to bother with saying please.

Chapter 2
The Game

"We are going to play a Please Day game," Mrs. Clover said. "The winner will be any bunny who says please perfectly all day long.

That means saying please every time you ask for anything."

Hopper decided to win the Please Day game.

This should be easy, he thought.

But remembering to say please every time
you ask for something isn't easy.
Mrs. Clover's class played basketball
during gym.
It was a very exciting game!
Marigold got near the basket.
She shouted, "Pass the ball to me!"

Everybunny froze.

Corny stopped dribbling.
Suddenly, Marigold realized her mistake.
"Oh, no, I forgot to say please!"

Hopper felt sorry for Marigold.
He was determined not to make the
same mistake.

Chapter 3
The Surprise Bonus

"May I please write on the blackboard?"
Hopper asked later.
Hopper loved to write on the board.
Mrs. Clover smiled. She let him write all
the math problems.

In the cafeteria, Snowball asked, "May I have the big brownie?"
"You forgot the magic word!" Corny exclaimed.
Hopper added, "You should have said, 'May I *please* have the big brownie?'"
The cafeteria bunny smiled.
Then she gave Hopper the big brownie.
Hopper was beginning to like saying please!

At the library, Mrs. Pumpkin asked,
"Who wants to read this book?"
Milkweed's paw flew up. "May I?" he asked.
"Aren't you forgetting something?"
Mrs. Pumpkin asked.
Hopper raised his paw. "May I please have
the book?"
Mrs. Pumpkin smiled. "That's very
polite, Hopper."

Hopper let Milkweed have the book.
But Milkweed was out of the Please Day game.

In music class, Hopper struggled with
his scales.
"Let me show you," Lilac said.
Hopper's ears flew up. She'd forgotten
the magic word!

Lilac blushed. "Oops! I should have
said please."
Now even polite Lilac was out of the game.

Hopper kept saying please all day long.

And the strangest thing happened.

He started to think the word might
really *be* magic!

Chapter 4
The Winner!

"May I please have your attention?"
Mrs. Clover asked at the end of the day.
"Who remembered to say please all day?
If you did, please raise your paw now."
Hopper's paw flew up.
He looked around the room. He was the
only one!
Mrs. Clover smiled. "We have a winner."

Hopper felt very proud and happy.
He had won the game!
But Hopper kept saying please.

Corny wondered why Hopper was still saying please.

Hopper shrugged. "I like the way please makes everybunny smile."

"I noticed that, too," Corny said.

"But why?" Corny wondered.

Hopper said, "Nobunny likes to do what they're told. But they're happy to do what they're asked."

"That makes sense," Corny agreed.

"Besides," Hopper added. "I want to win the next Please Day game, too. I might as well practice."

Corny laughed.

"May I please come over to your house
after school?" he asked Hopper.

Maybe *he* would win the next game.

Then they both burst out laughing.